Tales of Journey

Inspire Young Minds with Timeless Tales

Dr. A.R.G.

ISBN
Paperback 978-9-33415-295-1
Hardcase 979-8-89610-752-1

Table of Contents

Foreword

Dear Young Readers,

Welcome to *Tales of Journey*! I'm so happy you're here to read these stories. Every story has something special to teach us, and I believe stories are one of the best ways to learn. They make learning fun and exciting, helping us understand the world, grow stronger, and face challenges bravely.

Education isn't only about what we learn in school. It's also about learning kindness, fairness, and resilience - the ability to keep going even when things are tough. Imagine if everyone learned these things! We'd have a world filled with people who create, share, and work together to make life better for everyone.

Stories also bring us closer. They remind us that, no matter who we are, we all share hopes, dreams, and feelings. Through stories, we learn to understand and care for one another.

As you read *Tales of Journey*, I hope each story inspires you to be curious, to ask questions, and to imagine new ideas. Let these tales be a start to your own journey of learning and growing. You have a wonderful adventure ahead—go explore!

With excitement,
Dr. A.R.G.

The Journey to Grandpa's

It was the first day of summer vacation, and the early morning sun cast a golden glow over the city of Guwahati. Inside their cozy army quarters, Captain Raghav was bustling around, making sure everything was in order. Today was a big day—he and his son, Ravi, were heading to Siliguri to visit Ravi's grandparents for the summer holidays.

Ravi, full of excitement, could hardly sit still. "Papa, are we really going to Grandpa's today?" he asked, hopping from room to room, his eyes wide with anticipation.

Captain Raghav, amused by his son's enthusiasm, gave him a warm smile. "Yes, Ravi. We're all set. Your ticket is ready, and we'll be on the train soon. Grandpa is waiting for you."

Ravi's mother, Aparna, stood by the door, watching the scene with a soft smile. As the chief doctor at the army hospital, her days were always busy. She handed Ravi a small, carefully packed bag. "I wish

I could come with you," she said, kneeling to give him a hug. "But I've got a lot of work at the hospital. Your father will drop you at Grandpa's house, and I'm sure you'll have a wonderful time."

Ravi's expression softened. "Will you come later, Mama?"

"I'll try, sweetheart," Aparna said, gently ruffling his hair. "But for now, you and Papa are going to have an adventure."

Captain Raghav glanced at his watch and picked up the bags. "Alright, time to go! The cab is waiting outside."

As they headed out the door, Ravi clutched his father's hand, the excitement bubbling up again. The cab ride to the railway station was a whirlwind of excitement for Ravi. He pressed his face against the window, watching the bustling streets of Guwahati fly by, the vendors, the honking cars, and the distant view of the mountains that seemed to go on forever.

When they arrived at the Guwahati Railway Station, the sound of whistling trains, vendors calling out, and the clattering of footsteps filled the air. Ravi's small hand clung tightly to his father's as they made their way through the crowded platform.

"Papa, which train are we taking?" Ravi asked, his voice a mix of excitement and awe as he glanced at the trains lined up along the tracks.

Captain Raghav pointed to a shiny blue train. 'That's our train, Ravi. We'll take it to New Jalpaiguri, and from there, we'll travel to Grandpa's village in Siliguri.

Ravi's face lit up as they boarded the train and found their seats. He quickly settled by the window, eagerly watching as the station buzzed with life. As the train began to move, the rhythmic clatter of wheels filled the air, and Ravi turned to his father, his eyes wide with curiosity.

"Papa, how long until we get to Grandpa's?" Ravi asked, snuggling closer to his father.

Captain Raghav chuckled, sensing the impatience in his son's voice. "It's a long journey, Ravi. But I have an idea to make the time fly by."

Ravi's eyes gleamed with curiosity. "What is it, Papa?"

Captain Raghav leaned back in his seat, his arm wrapped around Ravi's shoulders. "How about this? I'll tell you ten stories during the journey. Each one has a special lesson, and I promise they'll keep you entertained."

Ravi's smile grew wider. "Ten stories! Yes, please, Papa! Tell me the first one right now."

Captain Raghav looked out the window momentarily, the green fields of Assam rolling past them. He turned back to his son with a gentle smile. "Alright, Ravi. Let's begin with the first story, and it's all about patience…"

Story 1: The Little Bamboo and the Oak Tree

In the heart of a vibrant, green forest, where the air was fresh, and the trees whispered in the wind, a tiny **bamboo shoot** grew beside a towering **oak tree**. The oak stood tall and proud, with thick, sturdy branches that reached toward the sky. Every morning, the little bamboo would look up in awe.

"You're so big and strong, Oak Tree!" the bamboo said one day, its thin stem trembling slightly in the breeze. "How did you grow so tall? I'm so small and weak."

The oak tree chuckled, its leaves rustling softly. "It didn't happen overnight, little one," it replied in a deep, wise voice. "I've been standing here for many, many years. My roots run deep into the ground, and I've stretched my branches slowly, year after year. You must be patient."

"But I don't want to wait!" the bamboo replied, frustrated. "I want to grow tall now! Why should I stay so small for so long?"

The oak tree swayed gently, its massive branches creaking in the wind. "Patience, little bamboo," it said calmly. "True strength takes time. If you grow too quickly, you won't be strong enough to face the challenges that will come."

The bamboo huffed, shaking its slender leaves in frustration. "It's easy for you to say. You're already big and strong!"

The oak tree smiled kindly, its old bark creaking as it bent slightly toward the bamboo. "Let me tell you something, little one. I wasn't always this tall. I, too, was once small and weak. But I stood firm, even when the wind blew hard and the rains came down. Every day, I grew slowly but steadily. That's what made me strong."

The bamboo sighed. "But what if I can't grow tall like you? What if I break before I'm strong enough?"

The oak tree's leaves shimmered in the sunlight as it answered, "You won't break if you are patient. If you rush, you might bend too far too soon. But if you wait, you'll learn to bend with the wind and stand tall when the time is right."

Years passed, and the little bamboo, taking the oak's advice to heart, grew taller and stronger. One summer, a fierce storm rolled through the forest. The wind howled, the rain poured down, and all the trees swayed under the storm's power.

The mighty oak tree stood tall, but its thick branches groaned under the pressure, some even snapping off with loud cracks. The bamboo, on the other hand, bent with the wind. It swayed back and forth, its slim body bending low to the ground. But it did not snap. When the storm finally passed, the bamboo stood back up, tall and strong. Meanwhile, the oak had lost a few of its heaviest branches.

Though missing some of its limbs, the oak tree looked down at the bamboo with admiration. "Do you see now, little bamboo?" the oak asked. "Patience is strength. You didn't break because you took your time and learned to bend with the wind. You were stronger than the storm."

The bamboo smiled, finally understanding. "Thank you, Oak Tree. You were right. I didn't need to grow tall quickly. I just needed to be patient and grow stronger every day."

Moral: Patience is Strength

As the train rattled along the tracks, Ravi looked up at his father with wide eyes. "So, the bamboo was stronger than the oak, because it was patient?" he asked.

Captain Raghav smiled and nodded. "Yes, Ravi. Just like the bamboo, when we are patient and take our time to grow, we become stronger on the inside. Rushing only makes us fragile. True strength comes from being steady and learning through life's challenges."

Ravi thought about this for a moment, then smiled. "I guess it's okay if I don't grow up too fast."

Captain Raghav chuckled softly. "That's right, my boy. There's no need to hurry. Everything happens at the right time."

Ravi leaned his head against his father's shoulder, feeling warm and comforted. "What's the next story, Papa?"

Captain Raghav grinned, giving Ravi's hair a little ruffle. "The next story is about a brave young boy named Veeru, who learned the importance of standing up for what's right…"

Story 2: The Courage of Little Veeru

In a small, peaceful village nestled between green hills and golden rice fields, there lived a young boy named **Veeru**. He wasn't the tallest or the strongest, but everyone knew that Veeru had a heart as big as the sky. His sense of right and wrong shone as brightly as the morning sun, and his kindness warmed everyone he met.

One sunny afternoon, Veeru was playing near the village square with his friends when he noticed something unusual. Standing by the old village well was **Uncle Ramu**, the poor farmer, looking sad and defeated. His clothes were worn, and his children clung to his sides, their eyes filled with fear and worry.

Concerned, Veeru rushed over. "Uncle Ramu, why do you look so sad?" he asked, his small voice full of worry.

Ramu let out a heavy sigh, his tired eyes meeting Veeru's. "I borrowed money from **Sarpanch Rao**, but even after paying it back, he won't return my land. He says I still owe him, but I've given him everything. What can I do, Veeru? No one dares to speak against him."

Veeru's small fists clenched at his sides. He knew the Sarpanch was rich and powerful, and everyone in the village feared him. Sarpanch Rao controlled much of the land and often used his power to take more than what was fair. Veeru's heart ached for Uncle Ramu and his family. He knew what the Sarpanch was doing was wrong—he was taking what didn't belong to him.

That night, Veeru lay awake, staring at the ceiling of his small room. He couldn't stop thinking about Ramu's sad face and how unfair it all was. Tossing and turning, he finally sat up. **Someone has to speak up,** he thought. **Even if I'm just a boy, I can't stay silent.**

The next day, the village gathered at the Sarpanch's grand house for a meeting. The sun was blazing high in the sky, casting long shadows over the villagers. They stood in a circle around the Sarpanch's chair, listening as he boasted about his wealth and power.

Veeru stood at the back, his heart pounding in his chest. He knew this was his chance. Taking a deep breath, he pushed through the crowd and raised his hand high. "I have something to say!" he called out, his voice trembling slightly but growing stronger.

The villagers turned, surprised to see the young boy speaking out. **What's Veeru doing?** they whispered. **Is he really going to speak against the Sarpanch?**

Sarpanch Rao, sitting proudly on his grand chair, chuckled. "What do you want, little Veeru?" he sneered. "This is not a place for children."

Veeru's heart raced, but he stood his ground. "Sarpanch Rao, what you're doing to Uncle Ramu is wrong! He paid back what he owed, but you still won't return his land. That's unfair, and you know it!"

The crowd gasped. A boy, daring to challenge the most powerful man in the village! The Sarpanch's smile faded, and his eyes narrowed as he glared at Veeru.

"Do you know who you're talking to, boy?" the Sarpanch growled. "I am the head of this village!"

Veeru swallowed his fear but didn't back down. "Being the head of the village doesn't mean you can take from others," he said, his voice now steady and strong. "Uncle Ramu has no one to speak for him, so I'm speaking for him now. You have to return what is rightfully his."

A murmur ran through the crowd. The villagers, who had been silent and afraid of the Sarpanch for so long, began to whisper to each other. **If Veeru, just a boy, can speak up, maybe we can too.**

Sarpanch Rao shifted in his chair, uncomfortable for the first time. He had never been challenged before, least of all by a child. But now, with the villagers watching him closely, he knew he couldn't ignore Veeru's brave words.

Finally, the Sarpanch stood up, his face red with frustration. "Fine," he snapped, waving his hand dismissively. "Ramu will get his land back. But remember this, boy—you have made a powerful enemy today."

Veeru didn't flinch. He had done what was right, and nothing else mattered. As the crowd erupted in cheers, Uncle Ramu rushed forward, tears streaming down his face. "Thank you, Veeru," he said, his voice trembling with emotion. "You spoke for me when I couldn't. You gave me and my family hope."

Veeru smiled, his heart swelling with pride. "It was the right thing to do, Uncle Ramu. Everyone deserves to be treated fairly."

Moral: Speak up for those who cannot speak for themselves

As the train hummed along the tracks, Ravi sat up straight, his eyes wide with excitement. "Papa, Veeru was so brave! Even though he was just a boy, he stood up to the Sarpanch!"

Captain Raghav smiled and ruffled Ravi's hair. "Yes, my boy. Sometimes, the bravest thing you can do is speak up for those who can't. It doesn't matter how small or young you are—what matters is having the courage to do what's right."

Ravi's face lit up with determination. "I want to be brave like Veeru, Papa."

Captain Raghav grinned. "You already are, Ravi. Now, let's move on to the next story. It's about resilience, and how never giving up can help you achieve the impossible…"

Story 3: The Journey Across the Ocean

In a quiet village by the sea, there lived a young boy named **Arjun**. His father, the village chief, was known for his wisdom and kindness, always guiding the villagers with care. But now, he lay sick, his strength fading with each passing day.

The village healer shook his head, his face full of concern. "There's only one cure," he said. "A rare herb that grows on a distant island, far across the ocean. But it's dangerous—no one has ever crossed the stormy sea and made it to the island."

Arjun's heart ached as he looked at his father, weak and frail. "I will go," Arjun declared, his voice filled with determination. "I will sail across the ocean and find the herb."

The villagers gasped. "But Arjun, the sea is wild, and the storms are fierce! No one has ever made it back."

Arjun's mother, tears in her eyes, touched his arm. "Please, my son, it's too dangerous."

But Arjun stood tall, his eyes burning with resolve. "If I don't go, Father will never get better. I must try."

The next morning, before the sun had fully risen, Arjun packed a small bag and set off to the village dock. A small boat awaited him, bobbing gently on the waves. As he stepped onto the boat, the morning mist swirled around him. He looked out at the vast ocean, feeling a shiver of fear run down his spine, but he swallowed it down and pushed off from the shore. His father needed him, and he would not fail.

The sea stretched endlessly before him, and the waves grew higher as the hours passed. The boat rocked back and forth, and the wind began to howl. Arjun gripped the oars tightly, his muscles aching as he rowed against the growing storm.

"I must keep going," he whispered to himself, his father's face always in his mind.

As the sun dipped lower in the sky, the storm arrived in full force. Huge waves crashed against the boat, the wind howled like a wild beast, and rain poured down, drenching Arjun to the bone. His small boat was tossed around like a toy in the storm, and it took every ounce of strength Arjun had just to stay afloat. "I can't give up," he thought, even as his body screamed for rest.

Just when Arjun felt he could go no further, he saw it—a distant island, glowing faintly in the storm's darkness. The herb! His heart leaped with hope as he pushed forward, his arms burning with exhaustion. Finally, the boat reached the shore of the island, and Arjun stumbled onto the sand.

The island was wild and overgrown, but in the centre of it, under a giant tree, Arjun spotted the herb—a small, glowing plant that looked like a beacon of hope. His heart racing with relief, Arjun carefully picked the herb, knowing it was the only thing that could save his father.

But the journey wasn't over yet. As he returned to his boat, the storm raged even harder. Waves crashed over him, and at one point, his boat struck a rock, sending him tumbling into the water. For a moment, he felt like giving up. The sea was too strong, the storm too fierce.

But then he remembered his father's gentle smile, his kind eyes. "No," Arjun said aloud, his voice shaking but strong. "I won't give up. Not now."

With all the strength he had left, Arjun swam back to his boat, his fingers raw and his body trembling with exhaustion. He fought through the storm, rowing with everything he had, and finally, as the storm began to clear, he saw the lights of his village on the horizon.

The villagers, who had been waiting anxiously, rushed to meet him as he stumbled onto the shore, exhausted but triumphant. "I made it," Arjun gasped, holding up the herb. "I have the cure."

The healer quickly took the herb and prepared the medicine. Within days, Arjun's father began to recover, his strength returning bit by bit. The villagers looked at Arjun with newfound respect, their hearts full of awe at his bravery and resilience.

"You did it, Arjun," his father said, his voice still weak but full of pride. "You saved me."

Arjun smiled, his heart swelling with pride and relief. "I couldn't have done it without remembering everything you taught me, Father. Never give up, no matter how hard things get."

Moral: Resilience Inspires Others

Ravi's eyes sparkled with excitement as the train chugged along the tracks. "Papa, Arjun didn't give up, even when everything seemed impossible! He was so brave!"

Captain Raghav nodded, smiling at his son. "Yes, Ravi. When you keep going, even when it's hard, you not only achieve your own goals, but you inspire others to be strong, too. Arjun's resilience saved his father and showed the whole village what it means to never give up."

Ravi beamed with excitement. "I want to be as strong as Arjun!"

Captain Raghav chuckled. "You already are, my boy. Now, let's move on to the next story. This one is about fairness and why it's important to treat everyone equally…"

Story 4: The Fair Business of Suryapur

In the lively village of **Suryapur**, nestled high in the hills, there was always a hum of activity. The village was famous for its rich farmland, where the farmers grew the finest fruits and vegetables. The laughter of children playing and the sound of farmers working filled the air. But this year, the village was filled with tension. A new business venture was underway—a market to sell the village's farm products to other towns—and everyone was talking about it.

Leading the charge was **Ravi**, a young man known for his honesty and kindness. The village trusted him because of his fair dealings with everyone. He didn't come from a wealthy family like the **Patels**, who had dominated the business in Suryapur for years. **Patelji**, the current business leader, was an old, powerful man who often used his influence to make unfair deals, buying farm products at low prices and keeping the profits for himself. The farmers had lived in fear of him for years, but with Ravi stepping up to create a new market, they finally saw hope.

The villagers whispered among themselves, "Maybe Ravi can bring fairness back to Suryapur's business."

Ravi worked tirelessly, meeting every farmer and talking to every family. He didn't make grand promises, but he made one important pledge: "I will treat everyone fairly. No one will be more important than anyone else. We will all share the benefits."

But Patelji didn't like this at all. He saw Ravi's popularity growing, and fear crept into his heart. "If this boy succeeds, I'll lose control of the market," he thought bitterly. Patelji wasn't going to let that happen. He started spreading rumors. He paid people to say things like, "Ravi doesn't know how to run a business! He's too young and inexperienced."

Patelji also began offering bribes to some of the poorer farmers, giving them sacks of grain, new tools, and even money. "Sell your produce to me, and I'll take care of you," he promised with a sly grin.

Ravi knew what Patelji was doing, and it hurt him deeply. One evening, he sat on the steps of his home, his head in his hands. "How can I win if Patelji is playing so unfairly?" he whispered to himself. His father, a wise and calm man, came and sat beside him.

"Ravi," his father began, "fairness isn't about who has the most money or who talks the loudest. It's about trust. If you stay true to your word, the villagers will see that. Let Patelji play his games. In the end, fairness always wins."

Ravi's heart swelled with courage. He decided he wouldn't fight back with lies or tricks. Instead, he continued visiting the farmers, speaking honestly and from the heart. "I don't have wealth to offer," he told them, "but I have something much more valuable—fairness. If you trust me, I will make sure we all benefit equally."

As the opening day of the new market grew closer, the village buzzed with excitement. The night before, something terrible happened. Patelji's son, **Suraj**, sneaked around the village, offering farmers extra money to sell their goods to Patelji's market instead of Ravi's. But one brave villager, a young boy named **Ramu**, saw what was happening. He ran to Ravi's house and breathlessly told him, "Ravi bhaiya, they're trying to cheat! They're giving farmers extra money to sell to Patelji!"

Ravi's eyes widened. "We can't let them get away with this," he said, determined.

The next morning, just as the market was about to open, Ravi stood in the village square and spoke loudly for everyone to hear.

"My dear friends," he began, his voice clear and steady. "We have a choice today. We can choose fairness, or we can choose lies. I will never offer you money or bribes because those things don't last. But what I offer is much greater: a business where we all benefit equally, where everyone's voice matters."

The farmers, moved by Ravi's words, looked at each other and realized the truth. They saw through Patelji's tricks and knew in their hearts that only someone as fair as Ravi could bring peace and prosperity to Suryapur.

When the first day of the market ended, the whole village erupted in cheers—Ravi's market was a success! Patelji, fuming with anger, stormed out of the square, his unfair schemes defeated by Ravi's honesty.

Ravi stood before the villagers, his heart full of joy and gratitude. "This success isn't just mine," he said, smiling warmly. "It belongs to all of us. Together, we've built a business where fairness is the foundation of everything we do. A fair society is a strong society."

From that day on, Suryapur's farmers thrived under Ravi's leadership. The villagers trusted him because they knew he would always be fair, and in return, they built a community where everyone's hard work was valued.

Moral: Fairness Fosters Trust

As the train rumbled on, Ravi looked up at his father with wide eyes. "Papa, the farmers believed in Ravi because he was fair, even when others weren't."

Captain Raghav smiled, nodding. "Exactly, son. Fairness is more powerful than any bribe or trick. When we treat people fairly, we build trust, and that trust can overcome anything."

Ravi thought for a moment, tapping his chin thoughtfully. "So, does that mean being fair can make a whole village stronger?"

His father nodded. "Yes, fairness brings people together, just like it did in the village. And fairness isn't just about people; it's about how we treat the world around us too."

Ravi's eyes lit up. "Like in nature?"

Captain Raghav smiled again. "Exactly, Ravi. Speaking of nature, let me tell you a story about a very busy little bee who learned something important about health and balance…"

Story 5: The Busy Bee's Discovery

In a lush green meadow, filled with colourful flowers and the hum of buzzing insects, lived **Bea**, the busiest bee in the hive. Every day, Bea would fly out at the crack of dawn, collecting pollen faster than any of the other bees. While the other bees took breaks, sipped nectar, and rested their wings,

Bea kept working, never stopping, always trying to be the best.

One sunny morning, Bea zoomed past her friend **Milo the Butterfly** who was resting on a flower.

"Bea, slow down! You're always flying so fast," Milo called out, fluttering his wings lazily.

"I can't slow down!" Bea replied, buzzing frantically. "I have to collect more pollen than anyone else. There's no time to rest!"

Milo laughed. "But Bea, you need to rest! If you don't take care of yourself, you'll wear out your wings."

Bea ignored him and kept flying, faster and faster. "I'm strong! I don't need to rest," she thought.

Days passed, and Bea kept working harder than ever. But one afternoon, as she was zooming from flower to flower, something happened. Her wings began to feel heavy, and her tiny legs ached. Bea tried to keep flying, but her body was too tired. She crash-landed onto a flower, too exhausted to move.

As she lay there, breathing heavily, **Queen Bee** flew over to check on her. "Bea, you've been working too hard," the Queen said gently. "You haven't given yourself time to rest or eat properly. Remember, health is the most important thing. If you don't take care of your body, you won't be able to work at all."

Bea looked up at the Queen, feeling weak. "I just wanted to be the best," she whispered.

Queen Bee smiled kindly. "Being the best doesn't mean working yourself into exhaustion. It means balancing hard work with taking care of yourself. When you rest, eat well, and keep healthy, you'll be able to do more in the long run."

Bea thought about it for a moment and realized the Queen was right. From that day on, Bea made sure to take breaks, drink nectar, and rest her wings. She still worked hard, but now she felt stronger and happier than ever before.

Moral: Health is Wealth

Bea learned that taking care of herself made her even better at her job. When you stay healthy, you can achieve more and enjoy life to the fullest!

Ravi nodded, thinking about Bea's lesson. "So, being healthy helps you do everything better?"

Captain Raghav smiled. "That's right, Ravi. Whether you're a busy bee or a hardworking person, your health is your greatest wealth. When you feel good, you can focus and accomplish amazing things."

Ravi leaned back, looking out at the rolling hills passing by. "I guess learning is a bit like that too, right? If you keep learning, you get stronger in your mind."

His father's eyes twinkled. "Exactly, son! Learning is a journey that never ends, and it helps you grow wiser with every step. Speaking of learning, that reminds me of a story about two princes and their quest for knowledge…"

Story 6: The Two Princes and the Quest for Knowledge

Long ago, in the magical kingdom of **Samarth**, nestled between rolling hills and shimmering rivers, there lived two young princes—**Aryan** and **Varun**. The brothers were both brave, strong, and loved by all the villagers. But in one important way, they were very different.

Aryan, the younger prince, had a curious mind that never rested. He loved learning! Every morning, while the sun rose over the castle, Aryan would be deep in books, asking the wise scholars questions about the stars, how plants grow, and even the art of leading with kindness. To him, learning new things was like discovering hidden treasures.

On the other hand, **Varun**, the older prince, thought he didn't need to learn anything more. "Why should I waste time reading books?" he would say, puffing out his chest. "I'm already strong, and one day, I'll be king. That's all I need!" While Aryan studied with the royal teachers, Varun spent his time showing off his sword skills, racing his horse, and hunting in the forests.

One day, the wise old **King**, their father, called his sons to the throne room. "I am growing older," the king said. "One of you will soon take my place as ruler of Samarth. But first, I must know who is ready."

Aryan and Varun listened eagerly as the king continued. "I will give you both a task. Tomorrow, you will each go to a village far away that needs help. The prince who solves the village's problems wisely and fairly will be the next king."

The brothers exchanged glances. Varun smirked, confident in his strength. Aryan, meanwhile, thought about the challenge carefully. "It's not just about being brave. I have to be smart," he reminded himself.

The next morning, the two princes set off. Varun, in a hurry to show his power, galloped ahead on his horse, his sword gleaming in the sun. Aryan, however, took his time, gathering maps, scrolls, and advice from the kingdom's elders.

When Varun reached the village, he saw two big problems: the crops were dying because of a drought, and a band of mischievous thieves had been stealing from the villagers. Confidently, he drew his sword and called out to the thieves, "Stop your stealing, or face me in battle!"

The thieves, seeing Varun's fierce stance, ran away. Varun smiled, thinking he had won. "The thieves are gone!" he announced proudly. But the villagers didn't cheer. "What about our crops?" they asked. "We have no water to grow our food."

Varun scratched his head. "I chased away the thieves, but I don't know how to bring water back."

Meanwhile, when Aryan arrived at his village, he didn't rush into action. First, he sat with the village elders, asking them about their problems. "We used to have plenty of water," one elder explained, "but our river has dried up."

Aryan thought for a moment, then remembered something he had read in an ancient scroll. "There might be an underground well here, forgotten over the years," he said excitedly. Using his knowledge, Aryan helped the villagers dig deep into the earth until, at last, they found the old well! Freshwater began to flow, and the villagers cheered.

As for the thieves, Aryan didn't chase them away with swords. Instead, he met with their leader and asked, "Why do you steal from the villagers?" The leader, surprised by Aryan's kindness, explained that they had no food. "If you stop stealing and help the villagers farm, you'll have all the food you need," Aryan offered.

The thieves, moved by Aryan's wisdom, agreed to become the village's protectors, and peace returned to the land.

When the king visited both villages, he saw that while Varun had bravely chased the thieves away, the village still suffered from the drought. But in Aryan's village, there was fresh water, and the villagers lived in harmony with their new protectors.

The king smiled proudly at Aryan. "Strength alone is not enough to rule," he said. "Wisdom, learning, and fairness are what make a great king. Aryan, through your quest for knowledge, you have shown that education is a lifelong journey—and that journey has made you a true leader."

From that day on, Aryan continued to learn, never letting his thirst for knowledge fade, and the kingdom flourished under his wise rule.

Moral: Education is a Lifelong Journey

Ravi's eyes gleamed with excitement. "Papa, Aryan became a great king because he never stopped learning!"

Captain Raghav smiled and nodded. "Exactly, Ravi. Aryan knew that strength wasn't enough. Learning new things every day made him wiser and stronger. Education doesn't stop—it continues throughout life."

Ravi pondered for a moment. "I guess it's like doing your best at everything, not just learning, right? Like, always working hard and being responsible?"

Captain Raghav's face lit up. "That's right, Ravi! It's not just about learning—it's also about how we carry out our duties. Whether it's big or small, doing your job with dedication builds trust and respect. In fact, this reminds me of two courtiers in a king's fort and how they handled their responsibilities…"

Story 7: The Two Courtiers and the King's Trust

In the grand kingdom of **Rajgarh**, a magnificent fort stood proudly atop a hill, overlooking the village below. Inside the fort lived **King Virendra**, a wise and fair ruler who made sure his kingdom was happy and peaceful. To keep the kingdom running smoothly, the king relied on two trusted courtiers, **Harish** and **Raghav**, to manage important matters.

Harish, the first courtier, was known for his hard work and dedication. Every morning, Harish would wake up before the sun and arrive at the royal court bright and early. He always completed his work with care, believing that serving the kingdom wasn't just a job—it was an important responsibility.

On the other hand, **Raghav** was the complete opposite. He was often late, took long breaks, and preferred to wander around the beautiful gardens of the fort, chatting with anyone he could find. "Why should I work so hard?" Raghav would think. "I'm already getting paid, and I can take it easy."

One day, **King Virendra** called both courtiers to his royal chamber. "There is trouble in the village market," the king said. "Traders are upset because their goods are being stolen, and the villagers are worried. I want you both to investigate and report back to me."

Harish took the king's task very seriously. He hurried to the village, spoke with the traders, and listened to their concerns. He spent days gathering information, waking up early and working late into the night. Harish knew that his duty to the kingdom was important and that the villagers depended on him.

Meanwhile, Raghav thought of the king's task as just another excuse to relax. He strolled into the village lazily, ate sweets from the market stalls, and lounged under a shady tree. "Why should I work hard?" he thought. "The problem will solve itself." Raghav jotted down a few quick notes without much effort and headed back to the fort.

When they returned to the royal court, **King Virendra** called for their reports.

Harish stepped forward first, bowing respectfully. "Your Majesty," he began, "I have found that a group of thieves is stealing from the traders during the night. The villagers are scared, and the traders are losing their goods. I suggest increasing patrols and providing protection to keep the market safe."

The king nodded thoughtfully, impressed with Harish's dedication. "You have done well, Harish. You have served your duty to the kingdom with great care."

Next, it was **Raghav's** turn. He yawned as he handed over his flimsy report. "There's not much to worry about, Your Majesty," he said lazily. "The traders are just complaining over small things. I didn't find any major problems."

King Virendra frowned, sensing something was wrong. "Is this all, Raghav? Did you really investigate the situation carefully?" he asked, raising an eyebrow.

Raghav shrugged. "I did what I could, but there's no need to make a big fuss over it."

The king's eyes narrowed. "Raghav, your lack of dedication is clear in your words and work. Duty is not something you can take lightly. You have failed to serve your kingdom with honesty and care."

With a heavy heart, the king dismissed Raghav from his position, showing the court that laziness and dishonesty had no place in the kingdom. He then turned to Harish, smiling warmly.

"Harish," the king said, "your dedication has brought the real issues to light. You understand that duty is sacred, and for that, you will be rewarded."

Harish was promoted to a higher position, and the people of Rajgarh respected him even more. They knew that a man who treated his duty as a sacred responsibility brought peace and prosperity to the kingdom.

Moral: Duty is God

Ravi listened closely, his eyes wide with wonder. "Papa, Harish was rewarded because he worked hard and cared about his duty!"

Captain Raghav smiled. "Yes, Ravi. Harish understood that duty is not just a job—it's a responsibility. When we do our duty with sincerity, we honor not just ourselves but everyone who depends on us."

Ravi thought for a moment, then asked, "But what if someone can't do what others do, no matter how hard they try? What if they're just different?"

Captain Raghav gave a thoughtful nod. "That's a good question, Ravi. Sometimes, it's not about doing things the way everyone else does, but about finding your own strengths and embracing who you are. You don't have to be like everyone else to make a difference."

Ravi's eyes sparkled with curiosity. "Do you have a story about that?"

Captain Raghav smiled. "I do, actually. Let me tell you about a little turtle named Tara, who learned that sometimes, going at your own pace is the best way…"

Story 8: Tara the Turtle and the Swift Stream

In the heart of a peaceful forest, where the trees whispered in the breeze and the flowers swayed with every gust, there lived a little turtle named Tara.

Tara loved to explore, though she moved slowly, taking in the beauty of every leaf, pebble, and bug she came across. She was curious and thoughtful, always wondering about the world around her.

One bright morning, Tara's best friend, Chiku the Squirrel, came scampering over to her with excitement in his eyes.

"Tara! Tara!" Chiku squeaked, almost out of breath. "You won't believe what I found today—a new stream! It's the fastest, coolest stream in the whole forest, and all the animals are there, splashing and playing!"

Tara smiled warmly, though she wasn't sure about it. "That sounds fun, Chiku, but I'm not very fast. I can't zip around like you do."

Chiku hopped up and down, waving his paws. "Don't worry, Tara! I'll take you there. You'll love the cool water—it's perfect for a hot day like this!"

So, with Chiku leading the way, Tara followed at her own slow pace. Chiku darted ahead and then circled back, making sure Tara didn't get left behind. Soon, they arrived at the stream, and it was even more beautiful than Chiku had described. The water sparkled under the sun, rushing quickly over smooth rocks, and animals of all shapes and sizes were splashing and laughing.

Tara felt a little nervous but also excited. "Maybe I'll just dip my feet in," she thought, stepping carefully into the stream. But the moment her foot touched the water, the strong current pulled her off balance!

"Whoa!" Tara yelped, spinning and tumbling as the swift water carried her downstream. She flailed her little legs, trying to swim against the powerful current.

"Tara! Hold on!" Chiku called out, racing along the bank to keep up with her.

Tara's heart pounded as she struggled to stay afloat. The stream was much too fast for her small, steady legs. Just as she thought she was going to be swept away, she spotted a large, smooth rock in the middle of the stream. With all her strength, Tara paddled toward it and grabbed hold, clinging tightly.

Panting and exhausted, Tara perched on the rock, far from the safety of the riverbank. She wasn't sure what to do next.

Suddenly, a familiar, gentle voice called down to her. It was Maya the Owl, who always seemed to have the right advice. "Are you alright, Tara?" Maya asked kindly, gliding down on her soft wings.

Tara nodded but looked worried. "I'm safe for now, but I don't know how to get back. The water is too fast for me."

Maya smiled warmly. "Don't worry, Tara. I'll help you," she said as she carefully lifted Tara in her strong talons and carried her back to the riverbank.

Once Tara was back on solid ground, she sighed with relief. "Thank you, Maya," she said gratefully. "I thought I had to keep up with the other animals, but the stream was too fast for me."

Maya nodded wisely. "Tara, you don't need to rush or be like everyone else. You have your own special strengths. Just because the stream is right for Chiku doesn't mean it's right for you. There's no need to hurry to enjoy life—you do things at your own pace, and that's what makes you special."

Tara smiled. "I guess you're right, Maya. I'll take my time and enjoy things in my way."

That day, Tara learned an important lesson. While the fast, rushing stream wasn't for her, she could still enjoy life in her own way—exploring the forest slowly and appreciating all the small wonders others might miss in their haste.

From that day on, Tara never worried about trying to keep up with the faster animals. She embraced her own pace, and soon, the other animals started coming to her for advice, knowing that Tara the Turtle, with her slow and thoughtful approach, always had the best ideas.

Moral: Everyone Has Their Own Strengths

Ravi giggled as the train rattled on. "Papa, Tara didn't have to go fast like the others—she just needed to be herself!"

Captain Raghav smiled and nodded. "That's right, Ravi. Everyone has their own strengths, and we all do things differently. Just because someone else is fast doesn't mean you have to be. What's most important is recognizing your own strengths and using them."

Ravi leaned back thoughtfully. "So, does that mean it's not always about being the best or the fastest, but about doing your best in your own way?"

Captain Raghav's eyes gleamed with pride. "Exactly, son. And that reminds me of two farmers—Ramu and Shankar—who learned that putting in effort and doing your best always brings rewards, while taking shortcuts can lead to disappointment."

Ravi's curiosity was piqued. "What happened to them, Papa?"

Captain Raghav grinned. "Let me tell you the tale of Ramu and Shankar's farms…"

Story 9: The Tale of Ramu and Shankar's Farms

In the peaceful village of Sundarpur, surrounded by bright, green fields, lived two friendly farmers—Ramu and Shankar. Both of them owned farms right next to each other and had been growing crops for many years. But even though their farms were close together, the way they worked was very different.

Ramu was a hardworking man who loved taking care of his farm. Every morning, he would wake up with the sun, stretch his arms to the sky, and get to work. Ramu believed that the more time and care he put into his fields, the better his crops would grow. So, he would spend his days plowing the soil, planting seeds evenly, and watering his crops carefully.

On the other hand, Shankar, his neighbor, wasn't as hardworking. "Why should I work so hard?" Shankar would say to himself. "The rains will come, and everything will grow by itself!" He was often lazy, skipping important things like watering or pulling out weeds, thinking, "It doesn't really matter."

As the days went by, Ramu's fields flourished. His crops grew tall and healthy, with bright green leaves swaying in the breeze. Every day, Ramu would walk through his fields, checking each plant and making sure they were all happy. He even talked to his plants, saying, "Grow strong, little ones!" And they did!

But Shankar's fields weren't looking as good. His plants were wilting, their leaves drooping in the hot sun. Weeds had taken over his field because he hadn't removed them. Still, Shankar didn't worry. "It'll be fine," he told himself, not bothering to tend to his land.

One evening, Shankar walked over to Ramu's farm, and he was surprised by what he saw. Ramu's crops were lush, green, and beautiful, while his own fields looked dry and weak.

"How are your crops so much better than mine, Ramu?" Shankar asked, scratching his head in confusion.

Ramu smiled kindly and said, "Shankar, you reap what you sow. I've been taking care of my land, watering my crops, and pulling out weeds every day. But you've been neglecting yours, my friend. The effort you put in is what you get back."

Shankar shrugged, thinking that he could still fix it before harvest time. But when the harvest season finally came, the truth became clear. Ramu's fields were filled with golden, healthy crops, and his harvest was plentiful. The villagers praised him for his hard work, and Ramu had enough food and money to take care of his family for the whole year.

But Shankar's harvest was poor. His crops were small and weak, and he barely had enough to feed his family. Regret filled his heart as he realized how much he had lost because of his laziness.

One day, Shankar knocked on Ramu's door. "You were right, my friend," Shankar admitted. "I didn't take care of my farm, and now I'm paying the price. I see now that we truly do reap what we sow."

Ramu patted him on the back and said, "It's never too late to learn, Shankar. Next season, work hard and care for your land, and you'll see the rewards. It's the same with everything in life—what you give is what you get."

From that day forward, Shankar changed his ways. He began working diligently, just like Ramu, and the next year, both farmers enjoyed a bountiful harvest. They learned that hard work and dedication always bring great rewards.

Moral: You Reap What You Sow

Ravi nodded thoughtfully as the train chugged along. "Papa, Shankar didn't take care of his crops, so he didn't get a good harvest, right?"

Captain Raghav smiled and replied, "Exactly, Ravi. Just like in farming, life rewards you for the effort you put in. If you work hard and give your best, you'll see the benefits. But if you're careless, you might face the consequences."

Ravi looked out the window, watching the scenery pass by. "So, it's like if you don't give up and keep trying, you can achieve great things, even if it's hard at first?"

Captain Raghav nodded proudly. "That's right, Ravi. Perseverance is one of the most important things in life. In fact, let me tell you about a little bird named Cheeku, who learned that even when things seem impossible, hope and determination can help you soar to new heights…"

Story 10: Cheeku, the Little Bird Who Didn't Give Up

In the middle of a dense, magical forest, where tall trees stretched toward the sky and flowers bloomed in every color imaginable, lived a small bird named Cheeku. Cheeku was a bright little bird with beautiful yellow feathers that gleamed in the sunlight. But there was one thing Cheeku couldn't do—he couldn't fly. No matter how hard he tried, his wings were just too weak, and every time he flapped them, he would fall back to the ground.

High above, the other birds soared in the sky, flying through the clouds, their feathers catching the breeze. They swooped and played, but Cheeku could only watch from a branch below, feeling sad. "I'll never be able to fly like them," he sighed to himself, his little heart heavy with disappointment.

But Cheeku's grandmother, Nani, always believed in him. Nani was wise, with soft, fluffy feathers, and she had seen many things in her long life. One day, she hopped over to Cheeku, her eyes twinkling with warmth.

"Cheeku," she said gently, "don't lose hope. Sometimes things don't happen right away, but if you keep believing and trying, you'll get there."

Cheeku looked up at his grandmother with a sigh. "But Nani, I've tried and tried. What if I'm just not meant to fly?" he said, feeling discouraged.

Nani smiled and fluffed her feathers. "Hope is like the wind under your wings. You may not see it, but it's always there, helping you along the way. Don't give up, my dear. Keep trying, and trust that your time will come."

Cheeku thought about his grandmother's words. He didn't feel very hopeful, but Nani always seemed to know best. So, with determination, he decided to keep practicing. Every day, Cheeku would flap his little wings, trying to lift himself off the ground. He would get tired and fall many times, but Nani's words stayed in his heart. "Hope is like the wind under your wings," he would remind himself, and he kept trying.

Then, one stormy afternoon, something unexpected happened. Dark clouds rolled over the forest, and the wind began to howl through the trees. The other birds flew off quickly, escaping the storm. But Cheeku, still on the ground, wasn't able to fly to safety.

The wind grew stronger, pushing Cheeku toward the edge of a steep hill. He tried to grab onto the grass, but the ground was too slippery. "Help!" Cheeku chirped, his heart racing as the storm threatened to sweep him away.

Just as Cheeku thought he was about to be blown off the hill, he remembered Nani's words: "Hope is like the wind under your wings." With all his might, Cheeku flapped his little wings. At first, nothing happened, but he didn't stop. He kept trying, and slowly, the wind began to lift him. Cheeku flapped harder, and before he knew it, he was flying!

"I'm flying!" Cheeku chirped joyfully as the wind carried him higher and higher. The stormy wind that had once scared him had now become his friend, lifting him into the sky for the very first time.

When the storm finally passed, Cheeku landed safely on a tree branch, looking around in disbelief. He had done it! Even the big, strong birds were amazed by his courage and determination. They chirped and cheered for him, proud of the little bird who never gave up.

From that day on, Cheeku flew proudly with the other birds. Whenever things got tough, he remembered the lesson he had learned—hope had given him the strength to fly. It wasn't about how quickly he did it, but about never losing faith in himself. And every time Cheeku soared through the sky, he smiled, knowing that even when things seem impossible, hope often wins in the end.

Moral: Hope Often Wins

Ravi's eyes were wide with excitement as he listened to the story. "Papa, Cheeku never gave up, even when it was hard!"

Captain Raghav smiled, nodding. "Exactly, Ravi. No matter how tough things get, hope gives us the strength to keep going. And when we hold onto hope, we can achieve things we never thought possible."

A Journey Full of Stories

As the train chugged along, Ravi looked out the window, the golden light of the setting sun casting a warm glow over the passing fields and trees. His heart was full of wonder from all the stories his father had shared. The stories had been more than just tales—they had been lessons, each one teaching him something about life, about patience, fairness, bravery, and most of all, hope.

Ravi turned to his father, Captain Raghav, and smiled. "Papa, those stories were amazing! Each one was so different, but they all made me think about how I want to be when I grow up."

Captain Raghav chuckled softly and ruffled Ravi's hair. "That's the magic of stories, son. They can teach us important lessons without us even realizing it at first. And as you grow older, you'll carry these lessons with you, just like I did when my father told me stories on train rides long ago."

Ravi's eyes widened with surprise. "Grandpa told you stories too?"

Captain Raghav nodded, a thoughtful smile on his face. "Yes, he did. And just like I'm doing with you, he passed down these little treasures of wisdom. Now it's my turn to share them with you."

Ravi snuggled closer to his father. "I hope one day I can tell these stories to someone too."

"You will, Ravi," Captain Raghav said, his voice full of warmth. "And you'll add your own stories to the mix. Life is full of adventures, and with each one, there's a lesson to be learned."

The train's rhythmic sound lulled the forest and hills outside into a peaceful scene. Ravi felt cozy, his mind wandering over the ten stories that filled their journey. Each story felt like a piece of a puzzle, coming together to show him how to be patient, kind, brave, and true to himself.

As the train gently slowed to a stop, signaling that their journey was nearly over, Ravi held his father's hand tightly.

"Papa," Ravi said, his voice soft but filled with determination, "I'm going to remember these stories forever."

Captain Raghav smiled, his heart swelling with pride. "That's all I could ever hope for, Ravi. Life is one big journey, and with stories like these, you'll always have a compass to guide you."

The two sat together, watching the world go by as the train prepared to reach its final destination. Ravi felt a quiet peace in his heart, knowing that no matter where life took him, he would carry these stories—and the lessons they held—with him, always.

And so, with the end of their train ride in sight, the father and son leaned back, filled with a warmth that only comes from shared moments and the magic of storytelling.

Questions to Ponder

1. How did "Harish – The Courtier" inspire you to be a better person?

2. What did you feel when Arjun chose to go to the island? How would you have felt in his shoes?

3. If you could give a gift to one of the characters in the book, whom would it be and why?

4. Imagine you are a friend of Ravi in the fair business of Suryapur. How could you help him on his journey?

5.   Which story touched your heart the most, and why do you think it affected you so deeply?

6.   If Little Bamboo was feeling sad, what would you say to cheer him up?

7.   What dreams do you think Ravi might have for the future? How do they relate to your own dreams?

8.   If you could write a letter to Veeru, what advice or message would you want to give him?

9.   Which character would you want to spend a day with, and what activities would you do together?

10 What lessons about family and love did you
    learn from Arjun's journey across the ocean?

A Final Word for Readers

As you close this book, remember that stories are more than just words—they are gifts, carrying lessons that can guide you throughout life. No matter where your journey takes you, remember to be patient, fair, brave, and hopeful, just like Ravi learned from his father.

And one day, perhaps, you'll share these stories— or your own—with someone special, passing along the magic, one story at a time.

I'd Love to Hear from You!

Thank you for joining me on this incredible journey through the stories of Captain Raghav and his son Ravi. I hope these tales have not only entertained you but also sparked thoughts, conversations, and a deeper understanding of the values that make us all better people.

Your Thoughts Matter!

I am always looking to improve and make my stories more engaging and meaningful for readers like you. Whether you have feedback, a story of your own to share, or a suggestion for my next adventure, I'd love to hear from you!

Reach Out to Me:

Feel free to send your thoughts, feedback, or any questions directly to:

Email: gangadasuapadareddy@gmail.com
Email: contact@drapadareddy.com
Website: www.drapadareddy.com

Your insights are invaluable to me, and I look forward to hearing how the stories moved you or inspired you to dream big. Who knows? Your ideas might even inspire my next book!

Thank you once again for being a part of my storytelling journey.

Warm regards,

Dr. A.R.G

www.ingramcontent.com/pod-product-compliance
Lightning Source LLC
Chambersburg PA
CBHW051300160726
47994CB00003B/1257